MW01179020

.

© Peralt Montagut, 08330 Premia de Mar (Barcelona) Spain 1988

Printed in C.E.E.

Printing in Apipe, S.L.

The Sleeping

Beauty

Illustrated by Graham Percy

PERALT MONTAGUT
Publishers

There was once a king and queen who had been waiting for such a long time for a child. At last the queen had a baby girl and they were so happy that the king announced that after the christening there would be a great feast.

They invited all the fairies they could find
in the whole kingdom (they found
seven). These seven fairies
were made godmothers
to the little princess.

For each of the seven fairies the king had prepared
a gold casket containing a knife, fork and spoon
all of pure gold and set with diamonds and rubies.
These were placed around the table set for the feast.

One by one the fairies presented their magic gifts
to the princess.

The gift of the youngest fairy
was that she should be the most
beautiful person in the world;

the next, that she should
have the wit of an angel;

the third, that she should be
wonderfully graceful;

the fourth, that she
should dance perfectly;

the fifth, that she should
sing like a nightingale

and the sixth, that she
should play every kind
of music exquisitely.

Suddenly there swept into the room a grey and
ragged old woman. She was an evil old fairy
who everyone thought had died years ago so
she hadn't been invited to the christening or to
the feast.

When the wicked old fairy saw there was no place for her at the table and no gold casket for her from the king she shrieked and pointed angrily at the little princess.

"One day your hand will be pierced by a needle and you will die from the wound," she hissed.

At this the last of the seven good fairies came out
from behind the curtain and said quietly,
"Your majesties, your daughter will now surely
be pricked by a needle but she will not die. Instead
she will fall into a deep sleep and after a hundred
years a king's son will come and wake her."

So it was that the king decreed that no-one should ever use a needle. All the needles in the land were to be destroyed.

Sixteen years had passed when one day the young
princess, roaming through the vast castle, came
across a little room where an old woman sat
cheerfully sewing with her needle and thread.
She had never heard of the king's proclamation
against needles.

"What interesting work," said the young princess
"show me how that is done."
She picked up a needle .... and the needle straight
away pricked her hand. Just as the wicked old fairy
had wished upon her, she fell down in a swoon.

The king, remembering what the young fairy had
promised, carried the princess to the finest room
in the palace and laid her on a beautiful gold and
silver bed.

They sent for the fairy who had promised a long
sleep for the princess instead of death and she
came quickly in a magic chariot drawn by dragons.

Then she told the king of her plan. So that the
princess would not be alone when she awoke,
everyone in the castle except for the king and
queen would be put to sleep by a magic touch
and would not wake up until the princess did.

So everyone in the castle, wherever they were
and whatever they were doing, stopped and slept …

The king and queen went out to the people and
told them all that no-one in future was to enter
the castle.

Indeed it was now impossible to get near to the
castle for all around it there quickly grew up a
forest of magic trees and over the doors and
windows grew thick creepers and thorny vines.

After a hundred years were gone, a king's son
was passing by the overgrown castle. When he
stopped and got down from his horse, the thick
forest opened for him and the vines uncurled
from the great doors so that he could walk straight
into this strange place …
where everyone seemed to be asleep.

In the grand room above the courtyard he found
the beautiful young princess in her gold and
silver bed and he thought her so lovely that
he gave her a kiss.

With that kiss she awoke and while they talked
happily together the rest of the castle came back
to life too.

In the evening everyone felt so hungry that they all came together for a great supper and danced to some old but excellent music by the musicians who hadn't played for a hundred years.

The prince and princess, who loved one another very much, decided to marry the very next day.